I See

Joe Cepeda

I Like to Read®

HOLIDAY HOUSE • NEW YORK

I Like to Read® books, created by award-winning
picture book artists as well as talented newcomers,
instill confidence and the joy of reading in new readers.

We want to hear every new reader say, "I like to read!"

Visit our website for flash cards, activities, and more about the series:
www.holidayhouse.com/ILiketoRead
#ILTR
This book has been tested by an educational expert
and determined to be a guided reading level B.

I LIKE TO READ is a registered trademark of Holiday House Publishing, Inc.

Copyright © 2019 by Joe Cepeda
All Rights Reserved
HOLIDAY HOUSE is registered in the U.S. Patent and Trademark Office.
Printed and bound in March 2019 at Tien Wah Press, Johor Bahru, Johor, Malaysia.
The artwork was created with Corel Painter and Adobe Photoshop.
www.holidayhouse.com
First Edition
1 3 5 7 9 10 8 6 4 2
Library of Congress Cataloging-in-Publication Data

Names: Cepeda, Joe, author, illustrator.
Title: I see / Joe Cepeda.
Description: First edition.
New York : Holiday House,
[2019] | Series: I like to read Summary:
"An easy reader where a boy
sees insects and animals"-
- Provided by publisher.
Identifiers: LCCN 2018060596
ISBN 978-0-8234-4504-2 (hardcover)
Subjects: | CYAC: Insects--Fiction.
Animals--Fiction.
Classification: LCC PZ7.C3184 Iap 2019
DDC [E]--dc23
LC record available at
https://lccn.loc.gov/2018060596

For Elana

I see.

I see.

I see an ant.

I see.

I see a butterfly.

I see.

I see a snail.

I see.

I see eggs.

I see birds.

I see.

We see.